The Knight Who Could Knit

Written by Teresa Heapy

Illustrated by Davide Ortu

Collins

Once there was a knight named Nicholas, who liked to knit.
He was a super quick knitter.

He knitted scarves, hats and socks for many people.
He knitted jumpers, gloves and blankets for giants and bears.

Nicholas was good at measuring wool and tying knots.
He kept all his knitting in a knapsack.

Nicholas lived in a palace with lots of other knights.

Their job was to look after Queen Sharon, Princess Pam and Prince Sam.

"My knuckles are cold!" said Princess Pam.
"My knees are freezing!" said Prince Sam.
"My nose is icy!" said Queen Sharon.

Nicholas knitted gloves, socks and hats for the royal family.

The other knights made fun of Nicholas's knitting.

"Knights don't need knitting!" said a knight called Chris.

"We wear shiny armour and chain mail."

"No, it's not very like a knight to knit," scoffed a knight named Zach.

"You need to put down your needles and learn how to joust like the other knights."

Nicholas felt a bit sad, but he knew his knitting was needed.

Suddenly, there was a loud HOWL!

Nicholas, Chris and Zach looked in the air and saw a dragon heading in the direction of the palace!

She was unusually small.

"We can fight her!" yelled Zach, in a booming voice.

But the dragon took no notice of Zach.

She simply started gnawing at the palace.

"I will fight her!" boasted Chris, scornfully. "It will be my pleasure!"

"She doesn't scare me! I'll race you!" shouted Zach.

But the dragon was quite fierce.
"HELP!" yelled the knights.

The dragon chased them all to the tallest tower in the palace.

She gnawed at the palace again.

"She's wrecking the palace!" Chris yelled.

The dragon turned. She began to advance on the knights.

She got ready to pounce.

Zach winced. "We have no chance!" he said.
His knees knocked.

15

Nicholas knew what to do.

He knitted a super-long scarf in super-quick time.

The knights dropped the scarf out of the tower.
They all climbed down it.
"Good! We're safe!" sighed the knights.
But the dragon started to cry.

"What's wrong with her?" asked Sam.

"I think she's got toothache!" said Nicholas. "Gnawing must make her feel better."

"She needs to go to the chemist for some pills!" suggested Princess Pam.

"No, I know what she needs," cried Nicholas.

Quickly, Nicholas knitted a hat and scarf.

He climbed up the tower, and he wrapped the scarf round the dragon.

The dragon nuzzled him.

I think she feels better! She will stop gnawing now.

"Well done, Nicholas," gushed Queen Sharon.

"Don't mention it," he said, bashfully.

"You are quite a character, Nicholas," commented Zach.

"You have proved yourself a noble knight!" agreed Chris.

All the knights decided that knitting was excellent.
So now Nicholas runs a knitting school for knights.

A knitting knight

After reading

Letters and Sounds: Phase 5–6

Word count: 493

Focus phonemes: /n/ kn, gn /m/ mb /r/ wr /s/ c, ce /c/ x /zh/ s /sh/ ti, ci

Common exception words: of, to, are, said, do, once, their, people, beautiful, many, who, proved

Curriculum links: History; Design and Technology

National Curriculum learning objectives: Reading/word reading: apply phonic knowledge and skills as the route to decode words; read common exception words, noting unusual correspondences between spelling and sound and where these occur in the word; read other words of more than one syllable that contain taught GPCs; Reading/comprehension: understand both the books they can already read accurately and fluently and those they listen to by making inferences on the basis of what is being said and done

Developing fluency

- Your child may enjoy hearing you read the book.
- Ask your child to reread their favourite pages aloud. Encourage them to read expressively, using a surprised, excited or similar voice for sentences with exclamation marks.

Phonic practice

- Challenge your child to find and read aloud the words with the new graphemes being taught.
    - Ask them to find the /zh/ grapheme (as in "treasure") on page 3 (*measuring*) and page 10 (*unusually*).
    - Ask them to break the words down to identify the individual phonemes. (*m/ea/s/ur/ing, u/n/u/s/u/a/ll/y*)
- Challenge your child to identify two-letter graphemes for the /n/ sound on pages 12 and 13. (*gnawing, knights*)
    - Ask them to break the words down to identify all the graphemes. (*gn/aw/ing, kn/igh/t/s*)

Extending vocabulary

- Ask your child to think about the words used to show how characters speak.
    - Turn to page 8. Ask: What is the meaning of **scoffed**? (e.g. *mocked, made fun of, laughed at*)
    - Challenge your child to read Zach's words as if scoffing.
    - Turn to page 12. Ask: What is the meaning of **boasted**? (e.g. *showed off, bragged, gloated*) What is the meaning of **scornfully**? (e.g. *jeeringly, mockingly*)
    - Challenge your child to read Chris's words as if scornfully boasting.